Hello Kitty's Fall Surprise

by Kris Hirschmann
Illustrated by Sachiho Hino

SCHOLASTIC INC.

New York   Toronto   London   Auckland   Sydney
Mexico City   New Delhi   Hong Kong   Buenos Aires

ISBN-13: 978-0-545-06116-2
ISBN-10: 0-545-06116-4

12 11 10 9 8 7 6 5   9 10 11 12 13/0
Printed in the U.S.A.
First printing, October 2008

, and 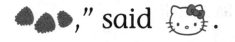 were playing

near the 🌳 one fall day.

The ☀ was shining.

The 🐱🐻🐰 had hiked all morning.

Now they wanted something

new to do.

"I know! Let's collect 🍃 and

🌰," said 🐱.

"Great idea!" said 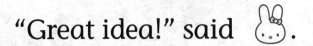.

All of the 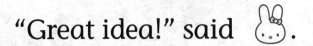 started picking

up colorful 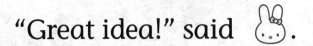 and prickly 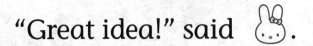.

They put them in 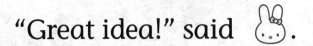's 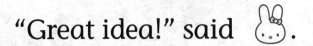.

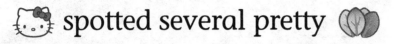 spotted several pretty 🍃🍃

lying together. She picked

up the 🍃🍃.

Under the 🍃🍃 was a big

pile of 🌰.

"Come and see what I found," she

called to her 🐻🐰.

🐻 and 🐰 ran over to 🐱.

"Oooh, 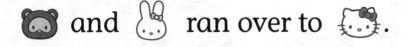!" they cried.

"These are great!" said 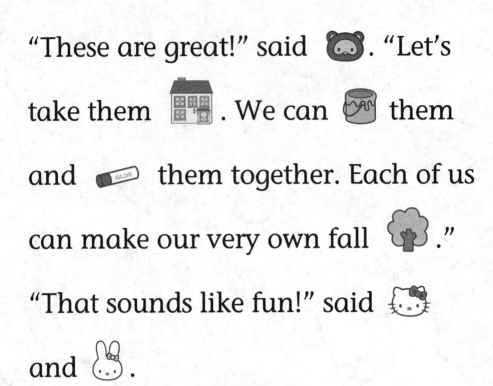. "Let's take them 🏠. We can 🪣 them and ⟨GLUE⟩ them together. Each of us can make our very own fall 🌳."

"That sounds like fun!" said 🐱 and 🐰.

Everyone helped put the 🌰 into 🐱's 🎒 along with the 🍃 and 🍂.

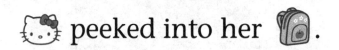

 peeked into her 🎒.

"That's a lot of 🌰. But it would

be fun to have even more," she said.

"Let's look for some!" said Kathy.

The 🐻🐰 started to search. They

found several more piles of 🌰 .

They picked up the piles and put

them into 🐱's 🎒.

Just then 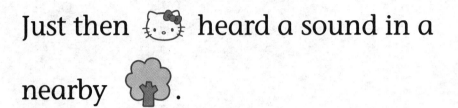 heard a sound in a

nearby 🌳.

She looked up and saw a 🐿️

sitting on a ✂️.

The 🐿️ looked at 🐱 with its

round brown 👀. It wiggled

its furry 🦴.

The 🐿️ looked very sad.

"What's wrong, little 🐿️?"

asked 🐱 .

The 🐿️ looked at the spot

where 🐱 had found the

first pile of 🌰 .

Then it looked at 🐱 and wiggled

its 👂 again.

Suddenly, 🐱 knew why the

🐿️ was upset.

"The 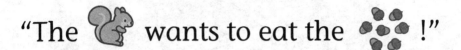 wants to eat the !" 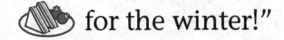 said. "We just collected all of its

 for the winter!"

"Oh, no!" cried .

"We have to give back the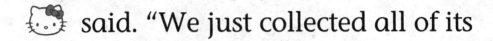

we collected," added .

"Let's find some more 🌰 for the 🐿," said 🎀.

🐰 saw some 🌰 under a 🌳.

🐻 found a whole bunch next to a 🪵.

🎀 spotted even more behind a 🪨.

The 🐻🐰🎀 piled all the 🌰 they found at the base of a 🌳.

Then they walked away, turned, and watched the 🐿.

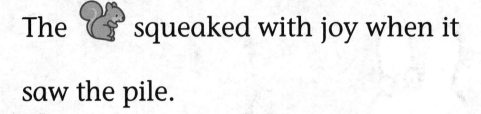

The 🐿 squeaked with joy when it

saw the pile.

It ran down the 🌳 and picked

up two 🌰 . It carried the 🌰

back up the 🌳 and put them

into a small 🪵 .

"This time, it's making sure its 🍱

is safe in its 🪹 !" 🐱 laughed.

Soon the busy 🐿 had carried all

of the 🌰 into its 🪵 .

The 🐿️ looked at the 🐻🐰.

It blinked its 👀 and waved its 🐾.

"The 🐿️ is happy," 🐰 said.

"How wonderful!"

"It *is* wonderful," agreed 🐱.

"Playing is fun, but helping new

🐱🐰 is even better. Our adventure

with  has made this the best fall

day ever!"

Did you spot all the picture clues in this Hello Kitty book?

Each picture clue is on a flash card. Ask a grown-up to cut out the flash cards. Then try reading the words on the backs of the cards. The pictures will be your clue.

Reading is fun with *Hello Kitty*!

woods	Hello Kitty
sun	Tracy
friends	Kathy

acorns	leaves
home	pinecones
paint	backpack

branch	glue
eyes	tree
tail	squirrel

rock	food
hole	bush
nest	log